ALIENS FOR DINNER

by
Stephanie Spinner

illustrated by **Steve Björkman**

A STEPPING STONE BOOK

Random House 🏠 New York

Library of Congress Cataloging-in-Publication Data
Spinner, Stephanie. Aliens for dinner / by Stephanie Spinner ;
illustrated by Steve Björkman. p cm. "A Stepping stone book."
SUMMARY: Aric the alien returns to Earth to help Richard Bickerstaff
save the world from an invasion of Dwilbs, pollution-loving aliens who
want to turn the planet into a toxic theme park.
ISBN 0-679-85858-X (pbk.). — ISBN 0-679-95858-4 (lib. bdg.)
[1. Extraterrestrial beings—Fiction. 2. Science Fiction.] I. Björkman,
Steve, ill. II. Title.
PZ7.S7567Al   1994   [Fic]—dc20   93-47105

Manufactured in the United States of America   19 18 17 16 15 14 13

This is for Jon.

—S. S.

1.

"Richard, have another egg roll."

"No thanks, Mom, I'm full," said Richard Bickerstaff glumly.

"How about another fried dumpling?" asked Bob Baxter. "They're really good—really good." He smiled encouragingly.

Richard didn't smile back. "I already said I'm full," he answered. This wasn't really true. He loved Chinese food, especially fried dumplings. But he liked to eat them with his mom, not with Bob Baxter, his mother's new boyfriend.

Richard wished Bob would go away. He was just a big boring guy with a moving van company. What did she see in him, anyway? Four dates, and now he was showing up for dinner! Richard didn't get it. In most other ways his mom was pretty smart.

"Well, I guess we'll have dessert then," said Mrs. Bickerstaff. "You're not too full for that, are you?"

"No, Mom," said Richard, brightening a little. As far as he was concerned, the whole point of eating dinner was dessert. "What are we having?"

"Ice cream," said Mrs. Bickerstaff. She and Bob started clearing the table. "And fortune cookies, of course." She pointed to the last white container on the table.

As she and Bob carried plates and chopsticks into the kitchen, Richard reached for the container. Funny. There was only one cookie inside—a big one. Should he open it, or save it for his mom?

But the fortune cookie seemed to have a mind of its own. As Richard watched, it began to rock back and forth on the table, first slowly, then faster and faster. Suddenly it burst into a dozen pieces. A tiny figure wrapped in a white paper strip struggled to stand up.

"Aric!" Richard's heart leaped. "Wow! It's great to see you!"

"It is good to see you also." Aric's voice was gruff, but his face was friendly. "As usual, though, it has not been easy getting here," he said, waving his tiny arms in the air. "I have heard of economy class, but this is ridiculous!"

Then he unwound the paper strip and read the message on it. "'Keep a clear head and you will save the day.' Hah!" he snorted. "Try keeping a clear head when you have just traveled 6.7 million miles in a fortune cookie!"

Richard smiled. Aric was a commander in the Interspace Brigade. His mission was to wipe out crime in the galaxy. He had appeared twice before, once in a cereal box, and once in a bag of microwave popcorn, to protect Earth from alien threats. Richard had helped him out both times, and both times Aric had complained a lot. Richard was used to it. He even kind of liked it.

"So, Aric," he said. "How come you're here? Are you on a mission? Is there another threat to Earth?" Richard's palms started sweating a little. He was one-third afraid and two-thirds excited. He knew Aric only came to Earth when there was trouble.

A serious look came over the tiny alien's face. But just as he was about to answer,

Richard's mother called, "Richard! Which would you like, Chocolate Joy Ride or Peanut Butter Fantasy?"

"Whoops!" Richard whispered to Aric. "We'd better go up to my room." He put the alien in his shirt pocket and headed for the stairs. "Uh, I'm not hungry after all, Mom," he called into the kitchen. "I think I'll go up and do my homework."

The minute Richard said this Mrs. Bickerstaff appeared in the doorway. She looked worried.

"No ice cream?" she asked. "Are you feeling all right, sweetie?" She put her palm against Richard's forehead.

"I'm fine, Mom," said Richard. "Really. I just forgot I have a lot of math to do."

"Well, all right," she said uncertainly. "We'll be up later to say good night. Won't we, Bob?"

"We sure will," said Bob. "We sure—" Before he'd finished, Richard was up the stairs and in his room.

2.

"Earth is once again in danger," said Aric the minute the door was closed. "A powerful group from the planet Dwilb has made it their target. They are businessmen—ruthless and greedy. They plan to take your planet over and make it into a theme park."

"What's so bad about that?" asked Richard. He liked theme parks, especially the kind with water slides.

"Let me describe what they have in mind," said Aric. "They will turn Earth into a carnival of litter, chemical waste, and gross, disgusting rides. They will call it Toxic Waste Funland. Then they will sell tickets to their fellow Dwilbs, and to every

10

other screaming, thrill-seeking, pollution-loving alien in the galaxy. By this time, you and your fellow Earthlings will be in their power. They plan to put you to work as guides. When the first tour ships arrive, Earth will be trashed. And you will be a slave in a funny hat."

"Yikes," said Richard. It all sounded pretty bad to him, especially the part about the funny hat.

"'Yikes' is right," said Aric. "On Dwilb they call Earth 'the Planet of Pollution.' And they are so sure of success that they have already started advertising. They are running commercials for Toxic Waste Weekends on the Intergalactic Shopping Network."

"But why us?" asked Richard. "Aren't there lots of other planets to choose from?"

"I hate to be the one to break this to you," said Aric. "But Earth is the most polluted planet in this sector of the galaxy."

Richard was surprised. He knew Earth was polluted. But was it bad enough to attract aliens?

"They like what they see here," said Aric. "The dirt, the waste, the chemicals. They think Earth will make them a fortune."

"Well, we can stop them, right, Aric?" asked Richard. "I mean, how bad can these guys be? Especially with a bogus name like Dwilbs! Who are they, anyway? How do we find them?"

Aric sat down on a stack of X-Men comics. "According to Brigade Intelligence, they are here, in your very town. A heavy source of pollution has drawn them—"

"I'll bet it's the chemical plant," said Richard. "They're being investigated for dumping toxic waste. Mom's working on the case." Richard's mother was a lawyer. Her specialty was the environment.

"Or maybe it's the oil spill," said Richard. Last week a tanker had leaked thousands of gallons of oil up the coast. Now the oil had reached Richard's town. There were news stories about it every day.

"Toxic waste *and* an oil spill?" said Aric.

"For Dwilbs, that's the perfect double feature."

"Well, so, let's get them," said Richard. "What do they look like?"

"They look like humans," said Aric. "And they say everything twice. This has a slightly hypnotic effect. The longer you spend with them, the stronger their hold over you gets."

"Really?" said Richard. "You know, I think I just met someone who says things twice. But I can't remember who."

"That is part of their power," said Aric. "You hear them, but you don't remember. And every time you hear them—"

There was a knock on the door.

"Quick! Behind the X-Men!" whispered Richard. Aric hid.

"Come in," called Richard.

Mrs. Bickerstaff and Bob stood in the doorway. "Bob's come to say good-bye to you, sweetie," said his mother.

Bob gave him a big smile and a little wave. "Good night, Richard," he said. "Good night, Richard."

3.

Breakfast the next morning was not a happy meal. Every time Richard thought of the way Bob had said good night he practically choked on his waffle. His mother was dating an alien! And she didn't even know it!

"Richard, honey, you're not eating," his mother said to him from across the table. She put down the Sunday paper. "I'm beginning to worry about you."

And I'm already worried about you, thought Richard. *Your new boyfriend probably has an antenna behind his ear.* But all he said was, "I'm okay, Mom. Just not too hungry."

"Try to eat a little," said his mother. Then something in the paper caught her eye. "I don't believe this!" she said. "The oil spill is getting bigger. And nobody seems to know why."

"Bad news!" Aric's voice boomed into Richard's head. Richard dropped his fork. He always forgot that the alien could speak to him this way—as if he were inside Richard's brain. Actually, he was inside Richard's pocket.

"It is the aliens," said Aric. "Pollution levels will rise sharply from now on. We must move with speed!"

Richard jumped up from the table. "Got to go, Mom," he said. "Think I'll take a ride on my bike."

"Be back in time for lunch, Richard," said his mother. "We're having company."

"Okay! I hear you," muttered Richard as he raced out the door. But he wasn't talking to his mother. He was talking to Aric, who was telling him to get to the oil spill—fast.

Richard hunched over his racing bars

and pedaled hard. Ten minutes later, he was at the beach. He dropped his bike and walked down a wooden ramp onto the sand. The beach was empty. Richard was surprised. Lately there were always people here, working to clean up the spill—including Henry and a bunch of kids from their class. Henry was the captain of the school's Green Patrol. He was really serious about the environment.

Richard pulled Aric out of his pocket. "Funny that nobody's here," he said.

"Look again," said Aric. He pointed at the water.

The sky was dark and overcast and the ocean was rough. At first all Richard saw

were the waves breaking, and beyond that the spill—a great big sludgy mass of black liquid floating on the green of the ocean. It smelled bad—like rotten eggs. It had never smelled this bad before, thought Richard. And it *did* look a lot bigger than it had just a few days ago.

Richard felt a little like choking. His eyes began to tear. He took off his glasses and wiped his eyes with his jacket sleeve. When he put his glasses back on, he finally saw what Aric was pointing at.

"Eeyow!" he gasped. "I don't believe it!" There, swimming right in the middle of the sludge, were four—no, five—guys! They were wearing bathing caps, and bobbing

up and down in the slick as if they were on a trampoline. They were totally covered with black, smelly oil. Not only that, they were slapping each other on the back and laughing!

"Meet the Dwilbs," said Aric grimly.

"Agh! Gross!" said Richard. He felt sick.

And then they spotted him. "Hi, there! Hi, there!" they called. "Come on in! Come on in!" Richard backed away.

"Aric!" he gasped. "How do we get rid of these guys? They're really scary!"

"Ah...Uh..." The little alien didn't really answer. Richard looked at him in alarm. "You *know* how to get rid of them, right?" Was it his imagination, or had Aric turned a deeper shade of pink?

"Of course I know," said Aric. "Or to be more precise, I *did* know. Before I had to travel in that torture chamber you Earthlings call a fortune cookie. The trip has done something to my memory."

"Oh no," moaned Richard. "You mean you forgot?" Richard's heart sank. Aric's memory was terrible.

"It will come to me," said Aric. "In time."

"Join us! Join us!" squawked the aliens again. "It's fun! It's fun!" Richard flinched. They sounded so cheerful! He wanted to leave, but it was hard to tear his eyes away from them. His feet felt as if they were planted in the sand.

"Richard!" boomed Aric. "Snap out of it! Let us go back to your dwelling! Now!" Richard forced himself to turn away.

"Do not worry," said Aric as Richard

pedaled home. "Things will get better—I swear by the Great Gazook."

But when Richard got home, things got worse. Bob showed up for lunch.

"Great chili, Harriet," he said. "Great chili." Then he started talking to Richard's mother about his business—Bob's Mighty Movers.

"A van for this, a truck for that—we'll get you there in no time flat!" was his motto. He was thinking of using it in a radio commercial. "So, what do you think?" he asked Mrs. Bickerstaff. "What do you think?"

"I like it! I like it!" she said.

Richard's jaw dropped. Was his mother turning into an alien, like Bob?

"Uh, Mom, may I be excused?" he asked hastily.

They hardly noticed when he left.

4.

On his way to school the next morning Richard kept thinking about the Dwilbs and the oil spill. Every time he did, he felt a little sick.

Just as he got to the bus stop something hit his leg. It was a piece of newspaper. Richard picked it up. What was it doing here? He looked around. Newspaper, empty paper cups, and crumpled brown paper bags were everywhere. Normally the streets were pretty clean. Not now.

Aric could read Richard's thoughts.

"Dwilbs," he said tersely. "They—" He stopped. Richard had come to a sudden halt. Then he groaned.

"What is it, boy?" The alien climbed out of Richard's pocket.

"Look, Aric. Over there!" They had come to the bus stop. A school bus had just pulled up and kids were climbing on. But Richard wasn't pointing at them. He was pointing to the bus's back fender.

Two pale, flabby men wearing straw porkpie hats were crouching behind the bus. They were sucking on its exhaust pipe.

"Agh!" exclaimed Richard. "They're inhaling the fumes! And nobody's paying any attention to them!" It was true. While the men took turns, kids just kept climbing onto the bus as if nothing was wrong.

Just then the men noticed him. "Try some?" one of them asked with a big smile. "Try some?"

"It's really delicious," said the other one. "Really delicious."

Richard stood there. Could they be telling the truth…?

"Run!" Aric's voice boomed in Richard's head. Richard ran.

He made it to school on time, but only because he ran the whole way. Once he was in class, though, his mind kept wandering.

He kept seeing the Dwilbs at the bus stop, and remembering how he almost couldn't move when they talked to him.

Richard wondered if he should talk to Henry. Henry knew all kinds of facts and figures about pollution—he had turned into a real expert. Maybe he could come up with an idea to stop the Dwilbs. *Somebody's got to*, thought Richard.

He decided to grab Henry the minute lunch period started. He and Henry always had lunch together, even though they didn't trade sandwiches anymore. These days Henry was eating raw vegetables and goat cheese.

Richard couldn't stand that healthy stuff. His idea of a good lunch was a Snickers bar and a jelly doughnut. Unfortunately, his mother didn't see things his way. She made him tuna on whole wheat.

When the bell rang Richard jumped to his feet. Mrs. Marks, his teacher, stood up too.

"Just a moment, class," she said. "Before you leave, I'd like some volunteers for beach cleanup." She looked expectantly at Henry. He always volunteered.

But Henry didn't raise his hand, or even look up. He just tapped his foot as if he was bored. Mrs. Marks looked around the classroom. No one moved.

"Green Patrol?" she said. "Don't you want to help?"

There was silence. "Not really," said Henry slowly. Then he laughed. So did everyone else.

Richard's mouth dropped open. What was going on? Why was Henry acting so weird?

"The Dwilbs are making progress." Aric sent the thought to Richard. He sounded worried.

"I don't understand you kids sometimes," said Mrs. Marks. She sighed. "All right. Class dismissed."

Richard grabbed his pack. Now it was more important than ever to talk to Henry. He hurried into the schoolyard. On warm days like today everyone liked to eat outside.

There were crowds of kids in the yard,

and they were all eating something Richard had never seen before. The stuff looked like soft ice cream or frozen yogurt, only it was a really dark color—almost black. It smelled bad, too. Richard wrinkled his nose. He couldn't quite tell what the smell was—just that it reminded him of something he didn't like.

Everyone was wolfing the stuff down. Richard was surprised to see that it came in Styrofoam cups, the kind nobody was supposed to use anymore. And kids were throwing the cups and plastic spoons on the ground when they were finished. *What is going on?* thought Richard.

"The Dwilbs have reached your schoolmates," Aric said. His voice was tense. "I do not like this. They are moving very quickly."

Then Richard saw Henry. His friend was making his way through the crowd to a little food cart at the end of the yard.

Richard followed him, kicking his way through piles of empty Styrofoam cups. There were about twenty kids at the cart. They were all shoving each other and waving dollar bills and yelling, "Get out of my way!" "I'm next!" "No, I am!"

Above their voices came the cries of the food vendors—two pale, flabby guys wearing red plastic Jughead hats. "Frozen Sludgies!" they squawked. "Frozen Sludgies! Come and get 'em! Come and get 'em!" The smell at the stand was strong—almost overpowering. With a shock, Richard realized it was the smell of rotten eggs—the smell of the oil slick.

He started to feel nauseous. Aliens! They were showing up everywhere! And what were frozen Sludgies? For a second Richard's mind stopped. The thought that came to him—that the aliens were selling a frozen dessert made from the oil slick—was so disgusting that he pushed it away.

Then he saw Henry buying a Sludgie from one of the aliens. "Don't eat it!" gasped Richard.

But Henry didn't hear him. As Richard watched, he began wolfing the mess down noisily, with his mouth open. He was acting as if he was in some kind of speed-eating contest. Sludge dribbled down his chin and

onto his shirt. Henry didn't seem to notice. He was too busy eating.

When he finished, he dropped his spoon and empty cup on the ground and headed back to the cart.

Richard's stomach knotted up. He felt dizzy. Maybe it was the smell of the Sludgies. Maybe it was the sight of his best friend acting like a total gross pig. Either way, it was too much for him.

"Henry!" said Richard. "Aren't you at least going to throw the cup in the trash?" Richard couldn't believe he was saying this. Henry was always the one who was telling Richard to eat right and clean up after himself.

Henry looked at him without saying anything. His face, usually so friendly, looked dull and suspicious.

"I mean, we should clean up after ourselves, right?" Richard added weakly.

"Duh. What for?" sneered Henry. Richard took a step backward. For once, he couldn't think of a single thing to say.

5.

Art was the last class of the day. Usually it was Richard's favorite. He always had a good time drawing spaceships and creatures from other galaxies. But not today. Today he caught himself sketching a flabby guy wearing a funny hat. *What am I doing?* he thought. *I hate the Dwilbs!* He threw down his pencil.

Just then the public address system came on with a loud screech. There was a violent thump against Richard's chest.

"What was that?" boomed Aric. He was in Richard's shirt pocket.

"Probably Principal Felshin." Richard sent the thought to Aric. "He likes to make announcements."

"Goo-oood...afternoo-ooon, girls and boys." The principal's voice was unhurried and dull, and he always took a really long time between words. Richard thought he sounded as if he was talking in slow motion.

"There are...a few important points...I would like to review with you this afternoon," said the principal. "The first...has to do with the use of the halls...as a meeting place. The halls, as you know,...are passageways designed for travel from one classroom to another. They are not...clubhouses...and they are not...living rooms. They are...conduits. And I hope you will look that word up.

"At any rate...to get back to my original point, I would like to...discourage any and all students...from passing time in the... hallways when they should be spending it to better effect. That is...moving briskly along to their next class, asking…pertinent questions of their devoted teachers, or, most important of all,…studying.

"My next point…is about the copy machine. As you know, a paper clip…left in the copier can do it…serious harm. It can jam the machine, thus…incapacitating it. I hope you will look that word up. This, in turn…can affect the workings of the entire…school. For what is a school without…a copy machine?

"I will answer that. It is a ship without…a sail. A car without…an engine. A refrigerator without…an ice-cube maker…"

Principal Felshin droned on and on. Richard, like most of the other kids in his class, didn't pay him any attention. Principal Felshin made two or three announcements a day, and they were all incredibly long and incredibly boring. Richard sometimes thought the principal should have a radio show late at night for people with insomnia. He could put anyone to sleep. The kids all called him The Sandman.

Richard felt his eyelids getting heavy.

He looked around the art room. A few kids were yawning. And Felshin had been talking for only two minutes!

Aric stirred in Richard's pocket again. "There is something about the way this man speaks..." he said. Principal Felshin's droning voice finally stopped and the PA system shut off with a loud buzz.

"You mean Felshin?" asked Richard. "What about him? He's totally boring."

"By the Great Gazook!" boomed Aric. "Boring! That's it!"

"What's it?" asked Richard. "What do

you mean?"

Just then the bell rang. School was over for the day. Suddenly the art room was wide awake again. Richard grabbed his pack, jumped out of his seat, and joined the crowd that was rushing out of the building.

"What's going on?" he said to Aric as soon as they were off the school grounds. "The suspense is killing me." He pulled Aric out of his pocket.

"I have just remembered something about the Dwilbs. Something crucial!" declared Aric.

"What is it?"

"There is a disease they catch very easily."

"A disease? What kind of disease?" asked Richard.

"It is called boredomitis," said Aric. "And it is fatal."

"I'm not sure I understand," said Richard. "You mean if they get bored they get sick and die?"

"In a nutshell, yes," said Aric. "They have very short attention spans. So they get bored very easily. And as soon as they do, they get boredomitis. But they don't die right away," added Aric. "The disease has four distinct stages."

"What are they?" asked Richard.

"Bored silly. Bored to tears. Bored stiff. And bored to death," said Aric.

"Really?" said Richard. He found himself grinning at the little alien. Suddenly he felt hopeful again. It was a great feeling.

"Really," said Aric. He grinned back.

"Then all we've got to do is bore them to death!" said Richard. "Right?"

"No!" said Aric. "We must bore them stiff. Then we can ship them back to Dwilb. Once they recover they will tell everyone on Dwilb how boring Earth is. No Dwilb will ever want to come here again."

Richard imitated the Dwilbs. "Too boring! Too boring!" he squawked.

"If I may say so," said Aric, "it is the perfect solution."

"Except for one thing," said Richard. "How are we going to do it?"

6.

At seven o'clock that evening, Richard heard his mother calling him down to dinner. "Coming, Mom," he called back, putting Aric in his pocket. He charged down to the dining room. There, to his surprise, was Bob. He was setting the table. Richard's good mood whooshed away like air out of a balloon.

"Hi, Richard. Good to see you! Good to see you!" said Bob.

Richard felt a twinge of fear. *Sorry I can't say the same, Mr. Alien Head*, he thought. He tried to smile politely. It came out like the face you make when you accidentally sit on something wet.

Bob just smiled back. His smile widened when Mrs. Bickerstaff came in carrying a huge bowl of spaghetti with tomato sauce.

Bet you'd like spaghetti with sludge sauce even better, thought Richard. Then he had a brilliant idea. If Bob was really a Dwilb, he could get boredomitis. All Richard had to do was bore him! Richard tried to keep a grin off his face. *How can I bore him silly?* he wondered.

"Try talking like Mr. Felshin," suggested Aric, from Richard's pocket. "That might work."

Great idea! thought Richard. He cleared his throat. "A really interesting thing…happened to me at school today," he began. "I thought I might…tell you about it." He spoke very slowly, just the way Mr. Felshin did.

"Sure, sweetie," said his mother. "What?"

"I was on my way to…homeroom," said Richard, dragging out every word. "And I got…really thirsty. So I decided to get a drink…of water. At the water fountain…in the hallway. But…when I got to the fountain…the bell rang…" Richard let his voice trail off. He twirled some spaghetti around on his fork.

"Well, so?" asked his mother.

Richard took a bite of spaghetti. "Well…there was hardly any water…coming out of the fountain," he said slowly.

"Just a tiny…drop. A…weeny…little…
dribble. It went drip…drip…drip…"

Richard stole a glance at Bob. Bob just
smiled at him and kept on eating. But his
mother was looking at him really oddly. Her
eyelids were drooping a little.

"Richard!" she said, yawning. "Get to
the point!"

"Well…" Richard sucked a few strands
of spaghetti off his fork as slowly as he

could. "I guess the point is...that I didn't get a drink of water...before homeroom. So I was...really thirsty...all during homeroom. And after homeroom..." Richard looked at Bob again. He was still busy eating.

Then he looked up. "Excuse me," he said to Richard. "But could you pass the spaghetti?" He turned to Richard's mother. She was yawning again. "This is delicious, Harriet," he said, beaming. "Delicious."

Look at them! Richard sent the thought to Aric. *My mom's falling asleep, and he's not bored at all!*

"Try something else," came the little alien's voice. "Ask for money. On Ganoob we consider that very boring."

I'll give it a shot, thought Richard. He cleared his throat again. "Mom," he said, in an extra-whiny voice. "Remember that sale I told you about at Mutant Splendor?" Mutant Splendor was a store in the mall that sold sci-fi stuff. Richard spent most of his allowance there. "It's a really great sale," Richard went on. "Three comics for the price of two."

"Richard! You have every comic book ever published!" said his mother. "Don't tell me you want more." His mother let Richard buy comics, but only one a week. He had a huge collection.

"Back issues of Space Lords of Gygrax!" said Richard. "I've got to have them, Mom. They're collector's items." Richard forgot about being boring. There really was a sale at Mutant Splendor, and he really wanted those comics. "And they'll be really valuable someday. I know they will."

His mother gave him a sharp look. She seemed wide awake now. "Why are you telling me this?" she asked.

"I just need a little of my allowance in advance," said Richard. "Only a few dollars, Mom. Please. Please?" His mother frowned, but for some reason Bob was smiling.

"Sorry," said his mother. "You're going to have to live without them. Now eat some more of your dinner, please."

"I used to love those Space Lords

comics," Bob said to Richard. "They were really fun. Really fun. I collected them, too."

"You did?" asked Richard. *On Dwilb?* he almost added, but he stopped himself.

"I did," said Bob. "As a matter of fact, I still have a few." He grinned. "The first Space Lords comics were so great. So great.

Especially numbers one to six. So I kept them."

Richard stared at Bob. "You mean you have the very first Space Lords comic ever published? *The Space Lords Creation Myth?*"

Bob nodded. Richard could hardly believe it. Even Mutant Splendor didn't have that one. It was really old.

"How about the second one?" asked Richard. "*Conquest of the Dranes?*"

Bob nodded again. "I think so," he said. He took another bite of spaghetti. "I could bring them over sometime if you like."

"Wow! That would be great!"

"It's a deal," said Bob. Then he turned to Richard's mother. "This is a wonderful meal, Harriet," he said. "Just wonderful." He and Mrs. Bickerstaff smiled at each other for a long time.

Richard put down his fork and sent a thought to Aric. "Aric! Maybe he's human after all! He didn't get bored. And besides, how could he have those comics if he was from Dwilb?"

Aric's voice came into Richard's head

loud and clear. "Face it, Richard," he said. "Bob is not an alien. He is just a man who says things twice—and who is in love with your mother."

Richard let the thought sink in. By the time his plate was clean he'd decided he was glad Bob wasn't a Dwilb. Maybe he did say things twice. Maybe he was a little boring. But someone as old as Bob who still had his Space Lords comics couldn't be that bad. He might even be okay.

As they finished up their spaghetti, Richard and Bob traded Space Lords stories. It was a lot of fun. When Bob came to the end of one called *Fearella, Space Empress*, Mrs. Bickerstaff stood up.

"It's getting late," she said with a yawn. "How about some dessert?"

"Sure, Mom," said Richard.

"Harriet! I guess this has been kind of boring for you," said Bob.

Mrs. Bickerstaff yawned again. "A little," she said. Then she smiled. "I'll get us some ice cream." Bob jumped up to help her.

Over dessert she mentioned that she and Bob were going out on Thursday. "The new recycling plant opens that night," she told Richard. "Bob is on the board of directors."

"I'm giving the guided tour," said Bob.

"Oh, is it open to the public?" asked Richard.

"Definitely," said Bob. "Definitely. We're having speeches, a tour, and a demonstration of the new equipment. I'm hoping we get a good turnout."

Aric had been quiet for a long time. Now he spoke up. "The Dwilbs hate recycling," he said. "If they know of this event, they will show up. They will try to wreck the place!"

Suddenly Richard knew what had to happen Thursday. He and Aric had to give the Dwilbs boredomitis!

"Can I come to the opening, too?" he asked his mother.

"Why, of course, sweetie," said Mrs. Bickerstaff.

7.

"We know we've got to bore them," said
Richard. "But that's all we know."

It was later that night, and Richard and
Aric were still trying to figure out how to
trap the Dwilbs. Richard was lying in bed.
The only light in the room came from Aric,
who gave off a faint pink glow in the dark.

"Bore them...bore them," mused Aric.

Richard smiled. "Speaking of boring, did
you see my mom when I was talking like
The Sandman? She practically fell asleep!"

"Yes," said Aric. "Your imitation of Mr.
Felshin was not bad."

Suddenly Richard sat up in bed. "That's it!" he exclaimed. "I mean, *he's* it! Mr. Felshin!"

"Mr. Felshin?"

"Our secret weapon! The most boring talker on the planet! If we can get him to talk to the Dwilbs—"

"By the Great Gazook!" said Aric. "You are right!" He was so excited that he glowed bright pink, like a neon sign. "That man can bore anyone into a deep, deathlike coma. His power is fearsome! The Dwilbs will not know what hit them!"

"So we've got to get him to the plant on Thursday," said Richard. "Because the Dwilbs will be there, right?"

"We will make sure of it," said Aric.

"How?" asked Richard.

"A mere detail," snapped Aric. "The important thing is to get Mr. Felshin to speak to them." He sat down in Richard's baseball glove.

"He must deliver a speech," said Aric. "A long, long speech. One that will give the Dwilbs a sudden, severe case of boredomitis. Once they are bored stiff," he went on,"the Brigade can ship them back to Dwilb. And Earth will be saved."

"Sounds great," said Richard. All at once he felt really tired. It was getting very late. "Can we figure the rest of this out tomorrow?" he asked sleepily.

"It has already been figured out," boomed Aric. "By a certain Ganoobian warrior of truly superior intelligence. Once again he has faced terrible odds on his mission. A ridiculous budget. Faulty communications. A ruthless enemy force. And once again he has overcome them—"

Aric was interrupted by a loud snort. Richard was sound asleep.

The next day Aric told Richard his plan. Phase One, he said, consisted of two phone calls. The first was to a woman named Marge La Farge, president of a recycling group called the Use It Againers. She was supposed to be the first speaker Thursday night.

On Tuesday after school, Richard dialed her number. Aric spoke into the telephone, doing an amazing imitation of Bob's voice.

"Marge. Marge," he said. "It's Bob. Listen, there's been a last minute change in the program on Thursday. Can you speak after the tour, instead of before?"

"Of course," said Marge, in a high, fluttery voice. "That will give me more time to get ready. Public speaking makes me so nervous."

"Great, Marge. Great. See you then." Aric signaled to Richard to hang up. Then he had him dial Bob's number.

"Hello, Bob. This is Marge," said Aric. Now his voice sounded like Marge crossed with a bullfrog. "I have some good news and some bad news, Bob. The bad news is that I won't be able to speak on Thursday. I have the flu." Aric honked loudly when he said this.

"Gee, that's a shame, Marge. A real shame," said Bob.

"The good news is that my wonderful friend Phil Felshin has agreed to take my place," croaked Aric. "You must have heard of Phil. He's the principal of the elementary school. And he'll be more than happy to open the evening with a few words. I've already asked him."

Richard held his breath. Had Bob heard what a terrible speaker Mr. Felshin was?

No. "Marge! Thanks! Thanks!" said Bob. "It's great that you got a pinch hitter. And on such short notice, too."

"Oh, think nothing of it," honked Aric. When he got off the phone he and Richard smiled at each other. So far, so good.

"And now, Phase Two," Aric said to Richard in his normal booming voice. "Are you ready to visit your principal?"

"I will make any sacrifice to save Earth," said Richard. "Even if it means talking to The Sandman. Let's go."

A few minutes later Richard and Aric were at school. The building was shadowy and quiet. Richard's footsteps, in his high-tops, made a loud scrunching noise as he walked down the empty hallway to Mr. Felshin's office.

The principal seemed very surprised when Richard knocked on his door.

His jaw dropped when Richard told him why he had come.

"The board of directors wants me to speak? Really?" Mr. Felshin flushed, and his voice shook just a little. Richard realized he was very pleased.

"They've heard about the talks you give

over the PA system," said Richard. "And
how all the kids like them so much."
Richard crossed his fingers inside his pock-
ets. He wasn't used to lying.

"They heard you talk about important
stuff," Richard went on. "Like not being
wasteful and respecting the environment
and stuff. So they thought you'd be perfect.
It's Thursday night at eight."

"Thursday?" Mr. Felshin frowned.
"Goodness...I don't know. My wife,
Edwina, and I...attend our ballroom danc-
ing class on Thursdays."

"Oh, no!" gasped Richard. It had never
occurred to him that Mr. Felshin might not
be able to make it. This was a disaster!

He beamed a thought to Aric. *What do I
do now?*

But Aric was silent. Richard was on his
own.

"But—this is for such a good cause,"
said Richard. He started sweating. "It's
important. I mean, it's important in a
major way, sir. The board members know
what a good influence you are on your stu-

dents. I think they're depending on you. I really do!" Richard's voice broke. He was ready to get down on his knees.

"Besides," he said, "you can have all the time you like and talk about anything!" *No matter how incredibly boring it is*, he wanted to add. But he didn't.

"Well…" Mr. Felshin picked up a pencil and put it down. He took a drink of water, which made his bow tie wiggle. Richard held his breath.

"Well…all right," said Mr. Felshin finally. "I suppose the tango can wait…And Edwina will understand…This is for a good cause, after all."

"Oh, thank you, sir," said Richard. His knees were shaking. "You'll never know what this means to everyone," he added.

And this time he was telling the absolute truth.

"I can't believe you fell asleep!" Richard said to Aric. It was later that day, and they were back in his room.

"I could not help it. He has the most

boring voice I have ever heard," said Aric. "It is more boring than Graxian folk singing. Or Drane poetry." The little alien was silent for a moment.

"Now," he said quietly, "we must discuss Phase Three."

"Phase Three?"

"We must make sure that the Dwilbs come to the recycling center on Thursday night," said Aric.

"How do we do that?"

"We must invite them." Something in Aric's voice made Richard uneasy. Then he got it.

"You mean, *I* have to invite them, don't you?" he said. Aric nodded. Richard's heart started pounding. He wanted to stay as far away from the Dwilbs as he could. But, he realized, Aric was right. They had to be sure the Dwilbs were there on Thursday. Otherwise their whole plan would fall apart.

"Remember, you are an honorary member of the Brigade," said Aric.

"How could I forget?" said Richard. He took a deep breath. "Let's go."

8.

Richard spotted the three Dwilbs in the bus station parking lot. They don't look mean, he thought. Big, yes. Nerdy, yes. But not mean. *So why am I shaking?* he wondered.

He forced himself to walk a little closer. They were at the back of the lot, where the buses were lined up, wearing baseball caps with fake ponytails. They were crouching close to the buses, breathing in exhaust fumes. They were smiling.

Richard's throat closed up. His hands, clutching a stack of flyers that announced the opening of the recycling center, were clammy. When the Dwilbs noticed him, he fought the urge to run.

"Hi! Hi!" they called together, jumping to their feet. Richard took another step toward them.

"Hi," he said. He had never been this close to them before. They smelled. Richard gagged. They smelled like a fish tank with dead fish in it.

"Hi," he managed to say again. "Come to the recycling plant tomorrow night?" He handed one of them a flyer and all of a sudden he was staring into three sets of Dwilbian eyes. Richard found himself thinking of a movie he had just seen with a scary *Tyrannosaurus rex* in it. The rex was a killer, and its eyes were like these—bright and empty.

"Wouldn't miss it! Wouldn't miss it!" said the Dwilbs.

"Great," said Richard. "Great! I, uh... I have to go," he added weakly.

"Stay with us. Stay with us," said the Dwilbs, leaning a little closer. Richard swallowed. They smelled horrible, but he couldn't seem to move.

"Richard!" Aric's voice was a shock. "Get away right now! Move it!"

Somehow, Richard moved it.

By eight o'clock on Thursday night the recyling plant was crowded. There were people sitting on rows of folding chairs, and people standing around talking. The noise was really loud. The plant had cement floors and a high ceiling, like a warehouse. A banner hung over the speaker's stand at the front of the room. "We ♥ recycling!" was painted on it in big green letters.

Richard sat near the back of the hall. He had come to the plant with his mother and Bob in Bob's van. He had told his mother he wanted to sit in back to watch out for Henry. But he was really watching for Dwilbs.

He checked the clock on the wall. 8:05. He checked the audience. No Dwilbs. Richard tried to stay calm, but worries dive-bombed his brain like mosquitoes. What if the Dwilbs didn't show up? What if *Mr. Felshin* didn't show up? So many things could go wrong!

Bob walked to the speaker's stand and picked up the microphone. There was an earsplitting screech, and the room went dark. Now the only light in the room was on Bob.

"Hello, hello," he said to the audience. "I'm Bob Baxter, and I'd like to welcome you here this evening…"

Bob introduced Mr. Felshin and Richard sighed a small sigh of relief. At least The Sandman had made it. Then he heard a shuffling noise from the back of the room. He turned.

There was no mistaking them, even in the dark. Thirteen oversized guys, all wearing hats with earflaps, were filing in. They sat down right behind Richard, so close he could smell them.

As Mr. Felshin stepped up to the stand, they all began whispering something. Richard could just make it out. "Are you ready? Are you ready?" They whispered it over and over again, rocking back and forth in their seats. Richard's heart thudded. The Dwilbs were whipping themselves into a frenzy. They were getting ready to strike!

"*Come on, Sandman!*" he wanted to scream. "*Get boring! Talk about the copy machine!*"

Mr. Felshin did even better. He cleared his throat and told everyone the title of his speech—"101 Ways to Reuse Plastic Bags."

"One," he said, in his slow, droning way. "Used plastic bags...make wonderful storage containers. They will hold everything...from paper clips...to rubberbands...to pushpins.

"Two," he went on. "Used plastic bags make excellent gloves. They can be used to pick up…all kinds of things…Things…you don't want to touch…with your bare hands. I am sure all you pet owners…know what I mean.

"Three," he said. "Used plastic bags make fine…emergency rain hats." He smiled. "Many is the time…I have used an old plastic bag…this way.

"Four…"

Richard heard a noise behind him. He turned. The Dwilbs were giggling—strange, high-pitched giggles that didn't fit at all with their big bodies. Then one of them stood up and began to bounce—up and down, up and down. The rest watched for a moment. Then they, too, jumped to their feet and started bouncing. Soon they were all bouncing together. They bounced so hard that the earflaps on their hats flew up and down, too, just like wings.

"Aric!" thought Richard. "It's working! They're bored silly!"

Richard heard a tiny snuffling noise from his shirt pocket. Aric was laughing. This had never happened before.

"You put your right foot in,
You take your right foot out,
You do the hokey pokey
And you shake it all about—"

The Dwilbs were lined up now, and singing the hokey pokey song. They had big goofy smiles on their faces. By the end of

the first line the whole audience was staring at them.

Mr. Felshin, though, kept right on talking. It was just like assembly, when he talked and talked and talked even though nobody was paying attention. "Six," he said. "Did you know that...you can sprout seeds...and grow plant cuttings...under

used plastic bags?" He didn't wait for an answer.

"Seven. You can blow them up like balloons...and then...pop them. This appeals to young children...probably because they make a very loud noise...almost like a pistol shot...when they are popped. The plastic bags, I mean...not the children." Mr. Felshin smiled at his little joke.

The Dwilbs, meanwhile, had stopped singing. They were still standing in line, but suddenly they looked surprised. Then they all started to cry.

"Yow!" Richard started to feel a little giddy. The Dwilbs were bored to tears! They definitely had boredomitis!

But they were attracting too much attention—sobbing and sniffling and blowing their noses so loudly that hardly anyone was listening to Mr. Felshin anymore. "Boo

hoo!" they cried. "Boo hoo hoo!" Their faces, once so weird and scary, were now dripping with tears.

"Aric! The audience is watching! How are we ever going to get these guys out of here? Everyone will see us!"

As he sent the thought to Aric, the Dwilbs stopped crying. They stood there quietly, their eyes wide and a little frightened.

"Ten," droned Mr. Felshin. "They make wonderful mitten liners for...tiny little hands..."

The Dwilbs didn't move. They stood absolutely still. Richard realized they were getting bored stiff.

"I will use the Ganoobian Mind Control Inducer." Aric's voice came into Richard's head.

"What's that?"

The little alien climbed onto Richard's shoulder. He was holding a silver object that looked like a tiny dog whistle. "A device that causes mass brainlock," he said. "Everyone within hearing will be affected."

"You mean they'll stop thinking?"

"Their minds will stop working. For eight Earth minutes—no more," said Aric. "And all memory of those eight minutes will be erased."

Richard was indignant. "How come you didn't use it before?" he demanded.

"It costs a small fortune," said Aric sternly. "And you know this mission is on a tight budget. Remember how I came here? In a cookie? Please do not complain to me!"

Richard knew there was no point in arguing. "All right, okay," he said. "Just hurry. They're already stiff as boards."

It was true. All thirteen Dwilbs stood there motionless. They looked like the life-size cardboard figures of actors that sometimes stand in movie lobbies.

"Hold your ears," said Aric. And then he blew.

9.

It was like the game Statues, thought Richard, when everybody freezes. Aric raised the Mind Control Inducer to his lips, and the audience froze. Now not only were the Dwilbs stiff, but everyone else was stiff, too. Mr. Felshin stood at the podium, mouth open. He couldn't say another word about plastic bags, at least for now. The scene was completely strange. For a moment Richard was frozen, too, staring at it.

"Hup! Hup!" Aric's voice boomed in the silence. "Snap out of it! We have aliens to move! Let us go!"

"Yes, master," said Richard. He couldn't believe how bossy Aric could be sometimes. "I obey." He picked up a bored-stiff Dwilb. To his surprise, the creature was very light. And now that it was stiff, it didn't smell so bad. He picked up a few more.

"To the parking lot!" commanded Aric. "To Bob's van!"

With Aric on his shoulder and four Dwilbs under each arm, Richard hurried outside. Bob's van was unlocked. Richard stashed the Dwilbs in the van, ran back inside to get the rest, and carried them out to the van, too.

"Now what?" Richard was panting.

"Get into the van," said Aric. "We are going to the beach."

Richard headed for the passenger door. "Not there!" barked Aric. "You are driving!"

"What?" Richard wasn't sure he'd heard right.

"You will guide the van. I will guide you," said Aric. "And hurry! You must be back at the center before the program ends. Your mother will be looking for you."

Richard climbed into the driver's seat. He fastened his seat belt. He could just reach the steering wheel. But his legs weren't long enough to touch the gas or the brakes. Richard had often dreamed of driving—usually a roaring red sports car—but now he felt like a midget.

"Keep your hands on the wheel and stay calm," said Aric. "I will do the rest."

Richard knew he didn't have any choice. He gripped the steering wheel and looked at Aric. The little pink alien was sitting on his shoulder, eyes closed. He made a high-pitched noise that rang in Richard's

ears and then traveled through his whole body. It felt like pins and needles, only better.

At the same instant the van's engine started thrumming. Richard's hands tightened on the wheel. The van was moving!

It shot out of the parking lot, lurched into a U-turn, and charged down a back street. It was going fast—too fast. The needle on the speedometer said seventy-five miles an hour!

"Slow down, Aric! We'll hit something,

or get stopped for speeding! They'll throw me in jail for life!"

"Oh, all right." Aric sounded grumpy, but he did slow down. Soon they were going along at forty-five miles an hour, and Richard's heart stopped racing. But then, about a mile from the beach, he heard a strange rustling in the back of the van. He looked in the rearview mirror.

Oh, no! The Dwilbs were moving! They were starting to unstiffen! Richard thought fast. Then he started talking just like Mr. Felshin.

"There is nothing like…a used plastic bag for sorting marbles," he said slowly. "Yellow in one bag. Green in another. Blue in…yet another. Then red. Then purple. And let's not forget multicolor marbles …They can go…in their own special plastic bag…."

He checked the mirror. The Dwilbs were stiff again. And it was a good thing, too. They were at the beach.

The engine stopped and Richard heard the slow rumble of breaking waves. He climbed out of the van. There were no lights on the beach and the night was foggy. He couldn't see much.

"We must get them onto the sand," said Aric.

We? thought Richard. But all he said was, "Yes, master." Then he carried the Dwilbs onto the beach.

"Stack them in a pile," Aric shouted over the crash of the waves. "The Brigade is ready for pickup."

But where is the Brigade? thought Richard. He peered up into the sky. At first, all he saw was fuzzy gray darkness. Then he spotted a tiny glowing speck far overhead. "Is that it?" he asked.

Before Aric could answer, the speck flashed and grew bright. Then it turned into a laser-thin orange beam, and streaked down through the sky to the sand. It found the stack of Dwilbs, danced, hummed, and crackled like lightning. The beam was so bright that Richard had to close his eyes.

When he opened them, the beam was gone. So were the Dwilbs.

"That is it," said Aric.

10.

"Richard, have another egg roll," said Mrs. Bickerstaff.

"Okay. Just one more," said Richard. Bob passed him the container. It was Friday night, and they were eating takeout Chinese food. Bob had brought it. He'd also brought over the first three Space Lords of Gygrax comic books, the ones from his collection. They looked totally cool. Richard couldn't wait to read them.

"So how was school today, sweetie?" asked Richard's mother.

A lot better, thought Richard. *Now that the Dwilbs are gone.* But all he said was, "Fine, Mom."

He smiled as he chewed on his egg roll. Life had definitely improved. No more Dwilbs in the schoolyard selling Sludgies. No more Dwilbs snorting exhaust fumes. No more Dwilbs pushing pollution. The streets looked cleaner. So did the beach. And Henry was acting like his old self again! He was back to eating weird vegetarian food and back to leading the Green Patrol. Richard had even volunteered in school today. Now he knew—they needed all the help they could get.

"How was your day?" he asked politely.

"Great!" said Mrs. Bickerstaff. "We finally got a trial date for the chemical dumping case—after all this time." She grinned. "Should be some trial," she said. "I can hardly wait. We're gonna whup those guys good!"

"Harriet! You're such a tiger!" said Bob admiringly.

Mrs. Bickerstaff blushed. "Well, you're

no slouch, either," she said. "Last night went so well. Everyone was impressed with the recycling center. And they liked the program too."

"They did. They did," said Bob. He put down his chopsticks. "There's one thing that puzzles me, though," he said.

"What's that?"

"Marge La Farge," said Bob. "She acted so strange after Phil Felshin's speech. So strange. Just marched right on stage and started talking."

"That *was* strange," said Richard's mother. "Didn't you tell me she had called saying she was too sick to speak?"

"That's right," said Bob. "That's right. Then she showed up. Completely healthy!" He gave a confused laugh. "I don't get it. I don't get it."

Richard figured he'd better change the subject. "Uh, Bob!" he said hastily. "Where did you put those Space Lords comics?" He jumped up. "I really can't wait to read them. Where are they? In the living room?" He headed for the door.

"Richard!" said his mother. "Where are

you going? We haven't even had dessert yet."

"Oh, that's okay, Mom," said Richard. "I can eat dessert later, can't I?"

Bob smiled. "They're on the coffee table, Richard," he said. "On the coffee table. Go ahead and read them. I want to help your mother clean up." He took Mrs. Bickerstaff's hand and they smiled at each other. "I'll be in later."

Now it was Richard's turn to blush. He hadn't seen his mom look at anyone that way for a long time. Little hearts were practically flying out of her eyes!

He hurried into the living room. There, just as Bob had said, were the Space Lords comics.

Richard kicked off his hightops and stretched out on the sofa. As he settled down to read the very first Space Lords comics ever published, he heard his mother and Bob laughing in the kitchen. He smiled. It was a nice sound.

The next day Mrs. Bickerstaff and Bob went out bike riding, so Richard and Aric had the kitchen to themselves. They were at the table, and Aric was climbing onto a salt-shaker. From here he would be beamed back to Ganoob.

"Don't you want to stay, even for the weekend?" asked Richard. He hated to see Aric go.

"I cannot," said the little alien. "Cosmic terrorism is at an all-time high. Entire galaxies are at risk. The Brigade calls. And besides, I miss Ingbar." Ingbar was Aric's girlfriend.

He stood up on the saltshaker. "Before I forget," he said, "I have something to give you. A token, to show the Brigade's appreciation for your excellent help." He held out his hand. In it was a small, shiny object.

Richard's mouth fell open. "The Mind Control Inducer? Aric! Are you kidding?"

"Most certainly not!" snapped the little alien. "And I expect you to use it with the utmost care! Remember that it will only cause brainlock for eight Earth minutes. And for Gazook's sake, remember how expensive it is! Save it for an emergency! I am not talking about a pop quiz, either!"

"Okay, okay," said Richard. Sometimes the way Aric read his mind was really embarrassing.

Suddenly the little alien started to fade. He raised a hand in farewell.

"Aric! Good-bye!" said Richard. "And thank you! Thank you for everything!"

"It was good to see you, Richard," said Aric, disappearing fast. "It is always good to see you."

And then he was gone.

About the Author

STEPHANIE SPINNER is the author of many books for children, including *Aliens for Breakfast* and *Aliens for Lunch*, which she wrote with her friend Jonathan Etra. She lives in New York City—"where there are lots of aliens," she insists, "especially the kind who say things twice."

About the Illustrator

STEVE BJÖRKMAN has been drawing since he was a boy, usually during class at school, but only when the teacher was boring. Some teachers told him it would never get him anywhere, but it did. Now he gets to draw for advertising, children's books, and greeting cards. He lives with his wife, three kids, a dog, cat, and hamster in Irvine, California.